HOCKEY DAYS

WRITTEN BY
Howard Shapiro

ILLUSTRATED BY
Kelly Brownlee

FOREWORD BY
Tom Cochrane

Thanks to all of my friends at BD&E, Todd Erkel, Borders, Joseph Beth Booksellers, The Pittsburgh Penguins, Renee Aiken, Bruce Springsteen, Big Country, Arcade Fire, U2, Peter Townshend, The Rolling Stones, David Terry/ AQUEDUCT, Lyle Hysen (rock and roll!), Stan Lee, Bob Kane, Kathy Cochrane, Jeff Jones, Gary Craig, Kenny Greer, Alan and Terry Robinson, Ernie the dog, Joel Bloom (and Carmel) and the Catanzarite Family.

Very special thanks to Kelly Brownlee for her creativity, vision, hard work and passion in bringing this story to life. You did a great job, Kelly, and I'll always be thankful to you! Steve Dora for his friendship and amazing design efforts... thanks for making me look good! My good friend Tom Cochrane (great songwriter, great performer, great friend and even better human being), my sister Jody Shapiro and my mom Alice Shapiro whose strength and character are second to none...I love you so much.

Extra special thanks to Gina, Sasha and Nikita, I love you three more than anything in the world.

This book is dedicated to the loving and everlasting memory of my Dad, Arnold Shapiro. He never missed a game of mine, took me to hockey practice at all hours of the day and night and who made every mile that we traveled together a fun and enjoyable one. He never thought that coaching or that coming to practices or games made him some kind of good parent, he simply loved to spend time with me. And that is a lesson more parents these days should think about. What I miss most of all is talking to him and simply hearing his voice everyday. Still, we all love and cherish our very fond memories of him. Si sentirà la tua mancanza e ti amo, il mio buon amico.

Hockey Days, A Supersonic Storybook Production, was filmed on location in Pittsburgh, PA, Mt. Forest and Toronto, Ontario Canada and Seattle, WA.

For more information please log onto www.howardshapiro.net. Please send your comments, questions or feedback to howard.shapiro@hotmail.net. Please check out my page on MySpace at http://www.myspace.com/howardshapiro

To order additional copies of this book, contact:
Supersonic Storybook Productions
1-866-520-4286
www.hockeydays.net
howard.shapiro@hotmail.com

₵OREWORD

Howard has the ability in his stories to express sentimentality in a way that is not maudlin but helps kids make the connection between life values, tradition and the games they love to play like hockey or baseball.

-Tom Cochrane

"Tom, will you be ready to go soon?" Dad asked. "We can't be late for the first game of the year."

"Don't worry, I'll be ready to go!" Tom said excitedly.

Tonight was his first DekHockey game of the year and the weather was perfect on this late-January afternoon, sunny but frigid. But warm or cold, snow or rain it didn't matter to Tom, he lived for hockey.

Tom heard the doorbell ring and a minute later Dad walked into the kitchen carrying a small box.

"Who's that from, Dad?" asked Tom.

"It's from your Grandmother," answered Dad.

Tom watched as Dad opened the box and looked inside. Dad's eyes got real wide and he pulled out a piece of paper.

"What does it say?" Tom asked. He sensed from seeing his face that he was a little stunned by what was in the box.

Dad read, "Dear Stuart: I found these while I was cleaning out your father's closet. He had them in a box with some of your trophies. I know these meant a great deal to him, so I wanted you to have them. Love, Mom."

He put the note down and pulled out a scuffed up orange ball that had some printing in black marker on it. He gazed at it for a second and then reached down and pulled out an old, yet very bright orange knit hat, which had an equally bright orange tassel on top.

The doorbell rang again and he put the hat and the ball back into the box and went to see who was at the door.

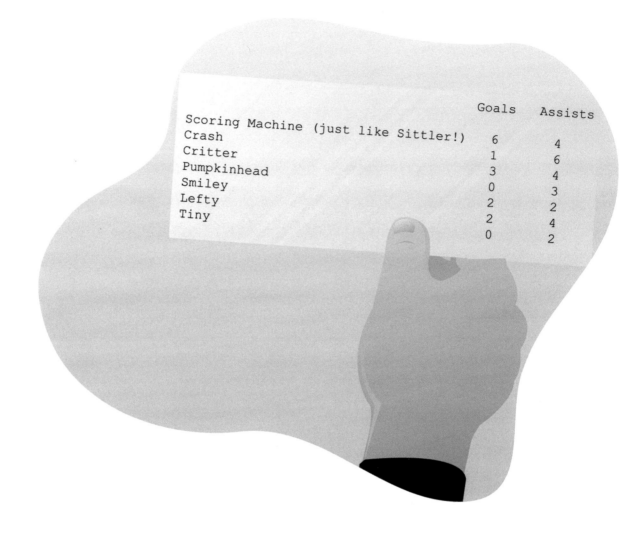

	Goals	Assists
Scoring Machine (just like Sittler!)	6	4
Crash	1	6
Critter	3	4
Pumpkinhead	0	3
Smiley	2	2
Lefty	2	4
Tiny	0	2

As Dad shuffled by, Tom walked over to the box and looked inside. He pulled out the ball and the orange hat and underneath it was a piece of paper. It read "FAIRVIEW 15 IRONDALE 14" and below that it had names on one side and two numbers on the other side. What stood out to him were the names: Scoring Machine, Crash, Critter and Pumpkinhead... he wondered, who were those guys?

He took out the orange ball. It read "Stuart Leonard game winner vs. Irondale, 2/22/1979."

"Pretty cool, huh?" Dad asked as he stood in the doorway.

"Yeah, you got the game ball," Tom said. "There was a piece of paper in there with a score and some names and numbers. Who were those guys and why'd they all have nicknames?" Tom asked.

"It was just more fun to call guys by their nicknames, rather than their real names. The guys gave me the nickname Scoring Machine which was cooler than Stuart, and Critter, well, he just looked like a critter," Dad said with a laugh. "Crash was my best friend. We'd play hockey in the alley between our houses after school and he'd say he was Randy Carlyle and I was The Fergie Flyer, George Ferguson who were our favorite Pittsburgh Penguins. We said that when we grew up, we were going to play in the big league for the Penguins."

"He and I used to play this old table hockey game and he could never stop my famous high post play. One game he got so frustrated, he made a fist and pounded the game so hard that he put a crack in the surface."

"I looked at him and we each started to laugh and, five minutes later, after he taped the game up, we started playing again. So, I called him Crash because his fist crashed into the game."

"So what happened in that Irondale game that made it so special?" Tom asked.

"We heard that those guys always wore black, that they painted their faces and that they played really, really rough," Dad said with a chuckle.

"Their big kid, Zambrano, was as tall as a Redwood tree and he even had a mustache at eleven years old! Another kid, Carter, had super long, curly hair, which covered his entire face and their goalie looked like a Volkswagen with a head. He took up about 98% of the net!"

"Were you scared of those guys?" Tom asked.

"We were," Dad said. "But right before we were about to start the game, your Grandad walked over and when I saw him I knew things would be ok. He actually gave me the orange hat before that game and told me that it was the hat he wore when he played shinny, which is pond hockey, as a kid. He said it was very special to him and that it would mean a lot to him if I wore it."

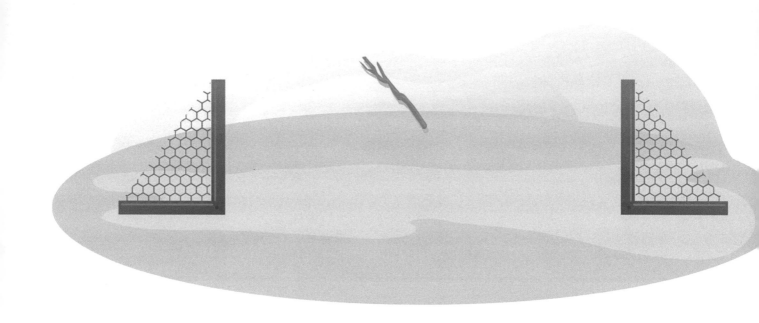

"Did he watch from the bleachers?" asked Tom.

"There were no bleachers. Things were a little different back in the 70's. We played in the back parking lot of Temple David. Your team plays on a nice surface with lights and a scoreboard. We used to nail a few two by fours together, nail some chicken wire on the back and call it a net. The centerline was a large tree branch and if the ball went into Mrs. Jones' yard, forget about getting it back."

"We'd play first team to fifteen won," Dad said. "But after I scored our fifteenth goal, we just kept saying next goal wins and we ended up doing that for at least another twenty five goals! And the Irondale guys turned out to be nice. Even Zambrano didn't look so big and bad when his Mom was dragging him by the ear to their station wagon so they could go home."

"But the best part of that day was walking home with your Grandad. He told me how playing hockey taught him so much about team work and discipline and he reminded me that, win or lose, the main thing was to have fun with my friends."

"I really miss Grandpa," Tom said quietly as he looked down.

"I know, buddy, me too," Dad said with a long sigh. "I can't believe it's been four months since he passed away." After taking a long, deep breath he continued, "It helps to talk about him and we just have to remember all of the good times we had with him and keep those fond memories alive."

Dad took the box back to his office. He set it down on his desk right next to a framed photo he had taken of his dad during their visit to the Hockey Hall of Fame in Toronto when he was ten years old. His dad was seated on a bench with his arms crossed and with a slight smile. He gently touched the photo and thought back to that trip and many of the good times they shared together over the years. He smiled at the memories of them talking and laughing together. He missed him so much, but thought what a great gift it had been to spend so much time together.

He then took the orange hat out of the box and walked downstairs. He spotted Tom's hockey equipment bag and placed the hat inside the bag.

Tom put his equipment bag down on the locker room floor. He unzipped the bag and looked inside and was very surprised to find the orange hat. He looked at it closely and then closed his eyes for a second and thought about his Grandad. The two of them had been very close; he always felt that Grandad understood him better than anyone else. He thought that by wearing the hat, maybe, it would feel like Grandad was close by, and not as far away as it seemed he was.

Dad stood quietly on the bleachers waiting for Tom and his team to come out and for the game to begin. He was the only adult in sight; all the other parents were in the lounge sipping coffee or hot chocolate. He glanced over and saw Tom walking out and he had the orange hat on. Tom motioned for his Dad.

"Dad," Tom said slowly. "Thanks for giving me the hat. Wearing it makes me feel like a part of Grandpa is still here with me."

"He loved you so much and would be very proud of you for carrying on his tradition," Dad said as he patted Tom on the shoulder.

A few minutes into the game, the ball squirted free and Tom picked it up at the centerline and ran in on the goalie, one on one. As he approached the goalie, the orange tassel flopping back and forth, Tom faked a shot to his right and then lifted the ball on his backhand into the open net as the goalie fell to the left! Tom's teammates cheered and as he went to celebrate the goal with them, he stopped and pointed first to his Dad and then up to the sky. Dad gave him a thumbs up and both he and Tom's Grandad, who was watching from heaven, smiled.